The Box

Written by Jill Eggleton
Illustrated by Rob Kiely

Rigby

Jack made a box house.
"I'm going to sleep
in this," he said.

"You can't sleep
in a box," said Mom.

Mom looked inside.
"I will sleep in here
for **one** night," she said.

Jack and Mom got into
their sleeping bags.
"This is cool," said Jack.
"I like sleeping in a box."

"I like sleeping in a bed,"
said Mom.

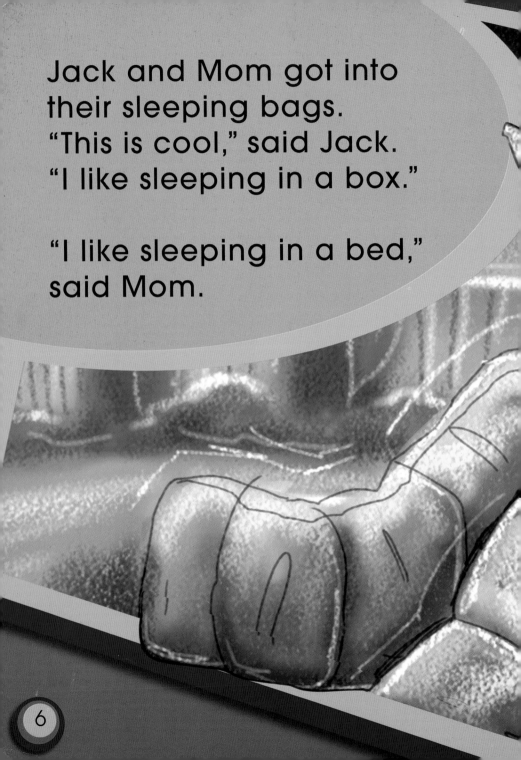

At one o'clock, a mouse ran over the box house.
Jack and Mom woke up.

At two o'clock, a possum ran over the box house.

They woke up again.

At three o'clock, a cat
jumped on the box house.

It went . . .
Meowww! Meowww!

"**Shoo!**" shouted Mom.
"We are sleeping in here!"

At four o'clock, Jack and
Mom woke up again.
It was raining.
The rain was coming
into the box house.

Drip! Drip! Drip!

"**Yuck!**" said Mom.
"I'm wet.
We can't stay out here!"

Jack and Mom went inside.
"Look at me," said Mom.
"I'm **not** sleeping
in a box again!"

A Plan

Guide Notes

> **Title: The Box House**
> **Stage:** Early (3) – Blue
>
> **Genre:** Fiction
> **Approach:** Guided Reading
> **Processes:** Thinking Critically, Exploring Language, Processing Information
> **Written and Visual Focus:** Plan, Speech Bubbles
> **Word Count:** 178

THINKING CRITICALLY
(sample questions)

- What do you think this story could be about? Look at the title and discuss.
- Look at pages 2 and 3. Why do you think Mom said Jack couldn't sleep in a box?
- Look at pages 4 and 5. Why do you think Jack wants to sleep in a box?
- Look at pages 6 and 7. Why do you think Mom likes to sleep in a bed?
- Look at pages 10 and 11. How do you know Mom is angry? Why do you think she is so angry?
- Look at pages 12 and 13. What do you think Mom and Jack could have done to protect themselves from the rain?

EXPLORING LANGUAGE

Terminology
Title, cover, illustrations, author, illustrator

Vocabulary
Interest words: sleeping bags, possum, box, house, night
High-frequency words: ran, again, their, one
Positional words: over, in, into, inside, on, up, out
Compound words: into, inside

Print Conventions
Capital letter for sentence beginnings and names (**M**om, **J**ack), periods, commas, exclamation marks, quotation marks, ellipsis